THE PARADISE FLYCATCHER

Deepak Dalal gave up a career in chemical engineering to write stories for children. He lives in Pune with his wife, two daughters, and several dogs and cats. He enjoys wildlife, nature and the outdoors. All his stories have a strong conservation theme. His earlier books in the VikramAditya adventure series are set in India's wilderness destinations. This is his third book in the Feather Tales series.

Krishna Bala Shenoi spends his days making things (mostly illustrations), procrastinating and exploring film. His artwork, spanning a variety of styles, has accompanied children's literature in books produced by esteemed publishing houses. He lives in Bangalore, where he plans to continue contributing to children's storytelling, imbuing his work with gentleness and a sense of wonder.

ALSO IN PUFFIN BY DEEPAK DALAL

Talon the Falcon
A Flamingo in My Garden

DEEPAK DALAL

The Paradise Flycatcher

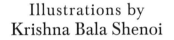

Illustrations by
Krishna Bala Shenoi

PUFFIN BOOKS

An imprint of Penguin Random House

PUFFIN BOOKS

USA | Canada | UK | Ireland | Australia
New Zealand | India | South Africa | China

Puffin Books is part of the Penguin Random House group of companies
whose addresses can be found at global.penguinrandomhouse.com

Published by Penguin Random House India Pvt. Ltd
7th Floor, Infinity Tower C, DLF Cyber City,
Gurgaon 122 002, Haryana, India

First published in Puffin Books by Penguin Random House India 2018

Copyright © Deepak Dalal 2018
Illustrations by Krishna Bala Shenoi

ISBN 9780143441748

Book design by Neelima P Aryan
Typeset in Baskerville MT Std by Manipal Digital Systems, Manipal
Printed at Replika Press Pvt. Ltd, India

www.penguin.co.in

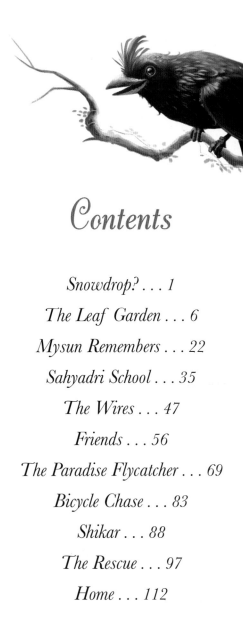

Contents

Snowdrop?

Mitalee had never felt this way before. There was a horrible tightness in her chest, as if a wall of bricks was pressing down on her. Her breathing had turned heavy and her heart was pounding. It was as if she had just completed a hundred-metre dash.

But Mitalee hadn't been running. That was the odd thing. She had been walking—unhurriedly at that, halting every now and then, staring up at the trees, parting bushes and rummaging through piles of leaves. It wasn't the kind of activity that would set anyone's pulse racing, yet her heart was hammering like a railway engine in her chest.

It was a perfect morning at the Rose Garden. The air was fresh and cool and the sun was shining from a clear blue sky. It was the kind of day that should have

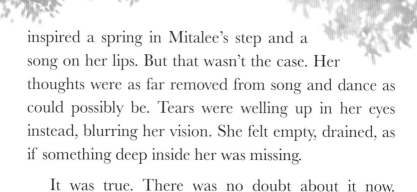

inspired a spring in Mitalee's step and a song on her lips. But that wasn't the case. Her thoughts were as far removed from song and dance as could possibly be. Tears were welling up in her eyes instead, blurring her vision. She felt empty, drained, as if something deep inside her was missing.

It was true. There was no doubt about it now. Snowdrop, the white-headed squirrel—the creature she adored, the one she loved most in the whole wide world—was missing.

It had all started the previous evening. Prickles of anxiety had stabbed her like sharp needles when she noticed Snowdrop's absence from the fountain. Every day, as the sun dipped in the sky, Snowdrop and the birds of the garden collected at the fountain to slake their thirst and exchange banter. This was a custom at the Rose Garden, a cherished tradition, and for as long as Mitalee could remember, Snowdrop had never missed an evening with his bird friends at the fountain.

The squirrel's absence had troubled Mitalee. Although she had stood rooted by her window, staring at the fountain, the furry head she had hoped to spot amongst the feathered ones of the birds hadn't turned up. The light had faded and the birds had flown to their roosts in the trees. Hunting for Snowdrop in the dark wasn't possible, so Mitalee had woken early, rising with the sun. She had searched the garden, examining each pile of leaves, each bed of flowers, each bush, each tree—but there was no trace of the squirrel.

Wow-Wow, Mitalee's dog, had accompanied her, padding at her feet as she roamed the garden. Strangely, Wow-Wow had started to whimper as her search had gone on. This had puzzled Mitalee. Could her dog have noticed the absence of the squirrel too? If he had, then his mournful response was peculiar, as the animals were sworn enemies. Snowdrop's favourite pastime was playing tricks on the slow-witted dog, whose dim brain was no match for the squirrel's cleverness. Mitalee wondered why the dog was whining instead of thumping his tail in celebration.

Surprisingly, Mitalee had found no sign of the birds either. This again was odd, as the day was just the kind that birds loved—with a blue, blue sky and a bright, warm sun. They should have been making merry with chatter and song. But this was not the case. A troubling silence bore down on the garden like a dark cloud.

The missing birds had prompted Mitalee to wonder if all the other garden creatures were absent too. But the thought had lasted barely a moment, because all about her was life and movement: damselflies hovered, flashing silken wings; butterflies flitted; grasshoppers bounced; bees buzzed; ants marched; caterpillars feasted; spiders spun their sticky webs; and lizards basked, enjoying the morning sun. The garden was its bright, happy self—except for the birds and her beloved Snowdrop.

After the long and fruitless search, Mitalee slumped on the grass beside the silent fountain. Wow-Wow curled at her feet, his snout buried between his paws, a steady whine escaping him. She stared dully at her mother's favourite bed of rose bushes. She no longer noticed the

bees as they flitted busily, transferring pollen from flower to flower. She didn't notice the sun as it climbed higher, nor did she notice its warmth when it shone brightly on her. It was only when the unfamiliar quiet of the garden was broken by the twittering of birds that Mitalee finally started. Wow-Wow looked up too. The sounds were unmistakable. The birds had returned but, curiously, their chatter issued from the neighbouring Leaf Garden.

The Leaf Garden

Mitalee hurried towards the chirping. She spotted the birds as she neared the wall that her Rose Garden shared with the Leaf Garden. There were many of them, a dozen . . . maybe more, she couldn't tell. For some reason they had flocked all over the bungalow in the Leaf Garden. This was unusual because birds are wary of humans. Typically, they collect in gardens or trees,

not around houses, where humans live. Yet this lot had selected the sprawling bungalow of the Leaf Garden. They were clustered all over it, perched on its roof, its veranda and its windows.

Mitalee loved birds. After Snowdrop—her first love—it was birds she was drawn to next. She could identify each and every bird in her garden and it was no surprise that she knew most of those that had gathered on the perches of the neighbouring bungalow too.

Up on the roof was the bulbul—the bird that was like a mother to Snowdrop. The fork-tailed bird with black feathers, flitting between the veranda and the roof, was the drongo. Beside him fluttered the yellow iora. The magpie-robin sat beside the bulbul and below, on the veranda ledge, were perched the bee-eater, the doves, the tailorbird and the tiny sunbird. There were two sparrows too—birds that Mitalee hadn't seen before.

As she watched, the sparrows hopped through the open doors of the bungalow. Although entering human homes was normal for sparrows—they are bold birds— Mitalee did not think this wise. The people who lived there weren't friendly and cared little for birds.

The gloom inside swallowed the sparrows. She was squinting, trying to spot them, when she was distracted by movement on the veranda. Two squirrels had hopped

on to the ledge. Mitalee recognized them instantly. They were Snowdrop's playmates, his best friends.

As Mitalee stared at the collection of creatures swarming the bungalow, the purpose of their gathering flashed to her. It wasn't a happy realization. It was an understanding that turned her cold all over, for now it was obvious that the worst had happened. The assembly of birds and squirrels indicated just one thing. Snowdrop the squirrel was indeed missing. All the creatures here were Snowdrop's friends. The only possible reason they

could have collected at the Leaf Garden's bungalow was to search for him.

One of the sparrows emerged from the house. Winging skyward, it alighted on the roof, beside the bulbul and the robin. Birds can't talk. That's what people say. But Mitalee was convinced they could, and from the manner the beaks of the birds twitched, it was clear to her that they were speaking to one another. The birds chattered softly. After a while, the sparrow flew to the open door. Moments later, the rest of the birds took to the air and, with Mitalee watching, every one of them winged into the bungalow. On the ground, the squirrels followed, scampering across the veranda into the shadowed interiors of the house.

Mitalee blinked. This couldn't be happening. Birds and squirrels do not enter human homes. It was unreal—as fanciful as her sprouting wings and flying like a bird. But as she looked on, their bold move—surprising as it was—started to make sense. She understood why the birds and the squirrels were risking their feathers and their fur. It was for their friend Snowdrop. They were searching for him. If someone had abducted the squirrel, the most likely culprit was Chintu, the boy who lived in the bungalow. Chintu hated Snowdrop. The extent of his dislike compared with Mitalee's affection for the squirrel. Just as much as Mitalee loved Snowdrop, Chintu detested him.

Chintu was a mean-tempered boy, and he possessed a catapult. For him, anything that lived in the trees was a target. He was dangerous; he could harm and hurt. The birds and squirrels were displaying exceptional loyalty and courage by entering his house.

Mitalee waited. She prayed that neither Chintu nor his equally nasty father was home. There was not a sound except for the rustling of leaves as a wind teased them. All she could see was darkness through the open door.

After several minutes, the stillness was shattered by a roar, quickly followed by yells, squeals and the squawking of birds.

'Oh no!' whispered Mitalee. The birds had been discovered! Chintu was home!

The first to exit the bungalow was the bee-eater, rocketing through the open door. The rest of the birds weren't far behind, shooting out of the bungalow. Behind them rushed three howling, whooping boys, all with catapults in their hands.

Blood rushed to Mitalee's head. 'Stop it!' she shouted. 'Don't shoot at the birds. Leave them alone!'

But the boys paid no heed, sprinting into the garden and firing at the birds.

'Shoot the bulbul!' cried Chintu, the biggest of the three. 'Get that bird—it's the leader. There it is, in the mango tree!'

The birds had scattered, many flying to neighbouring gardens. The bulbul, who was indeed their leader, had halted at the mango tree to look back and check on her friends. But on Chintu's command, all three catapults were turned on her. As stones thudded about her perch, she was forced to take to the air again. Instead of leaving the area, the bulbul winged skyward, high above the garden, till finally she hovered out of reach of the catapults.

The bulbul was worried. She had seen all the birds escape, but the squirrels were still inside the bungalow. They had panicked when the boys had surprised them and, instead of making for the door like the birds had done, fled deeper into the house.

Meanwhile, far below, on the ground, Mitalee's anger spilled over. Vaulting the boundary wall, she strode into the Leaf Garden, her dog at her heels. She confronted Chintu, waving a fist at him. 'Stop it, you bully! Stop it this instant, or I'll smack you!'

Chintu was a big, jowly boy. There was so much flesh on his face that it sagged in the form of a double chin. He lowered his catapult, smirking. 'You! You're going to hit me?' He put a hand on his chest. '*Save me*, guys— she's going to hit me!' Then he burst out laughing.

Arjun, the boy standing beside Chintu, made a face. 'Better get some first aid, Chintu,' he sniggered. 'Her hand will hurt so bad that we'll need to bandage it!'

'Ha ha ha!' laughed the boys.

Chintu pointed at Wow-Wow as he guffawed. 'Want to laugh some more, guys?' he said. 'Watch this.'

Bending, he made a vicious growling sound. Then, screwing up his face, he barked ferociously at the dog, who jumped backward, his ears flapping wildly. Whimpering, Wow-Wow dashed back to the wall and, leaping it, disappeared into the Rose Garden.

'Ha ha ha!' laughed the boys again.

Mitalee stood before Chintu defiantly, her chest heaving. Her eyes were bright like lamps.

Chintu winced. 'Hey! Don't you stare at me like that.'

Arjun suddenly cried, 'Look! Squirrels . . . there! They were hiding in the house all this time . . . Shoot them!'

From high above, the bulbul squawked in dismay. The squirrels couldn't have chosen a worse moment to emerge. The boys were standing right there, between the squirrels and the trees.

The squirrels dashed forward. The boys raised their catapults. Mitalee reacted fast—she flung herself on Chintu just as he released his stone, upsetting his aim. But the other boys fired unhindered. Luckily for the squirrels, their missiles thudded into the ground, erupting harmless clouds of dust.

'Drat!' hissed Arjun. 'What a time to run out of stones!'

But Maitreya, the third boy, had several in his pocket. Whipping one out, he took aim and fired.

'YAY!' yelled the boys.

Maitreya's aim was true. The smaller of the two squirrels uttered a terrible, heart-wrenching squeak. Mitalee's hands flew to her mouth.

Chintu's double chin bounced yo-yo-like as he and Arjun danced in glee. But

Maitreya, the boy whose missile had struck the squirrel, didn't participate in the celebrations. His catapult fell to the ground, and then, like Mitalee, he too pressed his hands to his mouth.

The squirrels continued towards the trees. The injured one was dragging its leg and its companion was keeping it company. At their hobbling pace, they were easy targets. Mitalee rushed forward, placing herself between the squirrels and the boys, shielding them from the catapults.

'GET THEM!' roared Chintu. Grabbing one of Maitreya's stones, he loaded his catapult. Arjun had already snatched one from the ground. He was ready, his slingshot pulled back. But as he was about to launch his projectile, a whirring sound descended from above, and he yelled when something sharp and hard pierced his skin.

It was the bulbul! Spotting the danger, the bird had dived and attacked the boy. Before Chintu could react, the bird pounced on him too, sinking her beak in his thick neck. The bulbul then shot back into the air.

Mitalee silently applauded the bird. The bulbul was brave and even now she was hovering above the boys, presenting herself as a target. Chintu and Arjun were

slinging stones skyward, but the intelligent bird stayed just out of reach.

Chintu was furious. 'Get that bird!' he howled. 'Bit me, huh? How dare it! I'm going to show it . . . I'll blast it out of the sky!'

Mitalee allowed herself a smile. The bulbul's plan had worked perfectly—the squirrels had disappeared into the thick foliage of the trees. The boys had been outwitted. Above, in the sky, the bulbul floated higher and winged her way out of the gardens.

'So much for your shooting skills,' scoffed Mitalee. 'You boys can't hit a door even if it's in front of you.'

Chintu glared at her. 'Shut your mouth, bird girl. We got that squirrel, didn't we?'

'No, you didn't,' said Mitalee. 'Neither did your friend Arjun. Even a blind man could do a better job than you two!' She spun around, turning to Maitreya. The boy flinched as her eyes grew wide and turned a smouldering red. 'And you! *You're* the one who shot the squirrel. Harmed a perfectly innocent animal. For what? Just fun? Did you hear the squirrel? Heard it howl? Did that scream make you happy? Did the pain you inflicted warm your cruel heart? *Did it?*'

The boy quivered. The intensity of Mitalee's gaze scorched him like the desert sun.

Mitalee ranted on. 'You had me fooled. The new boy in school. You were courteous and good at your studies—I thought you were a decent sort. But look at the company you have chosen! Now I know. You—'

Chintu interrupted, sneering, '*You*, bird girl, are the wrong company. Maitreya knows who his friends are. And they aren't birdbrained like you!'

'Yeah,' growled Arjun, 'who'd want a bird girl like you as a friend, huh? Only the sort that eats seeds, ha ha!'

Mitalee breathed heavily. 'You two deserve him as your friend. He's just right for you. Fits your type.

A coward—he shoots at defenceless animals, draws pleasure from hurting innocent creatures. You couldn't have found a better match!'

Mitalee wasn't watching Maitreya, but the boy winced at each of her barbed insults.

Mitalee wasn't finished. She faced Chintu, hands on her hips. 'Enough of this wretch of a friend of yours. I have more important matters to discuss with you. The white-headed squirrel is missing. He's been gone since yesterday. Where is he?'

Chintu made an elaborate gesture of searching his pockets. 'Nope,' he said, turning them inside out, 'no squirrel here.'

Chintu and Arjun clutched their sides, laughing. Maitreya did not take part in the merriment.

Mitalee glared at Chintu, her eyes turning larger and rounder, like marbles.

Chintu flinched. 'Hey! Stop it! I told you not to stare at me like that.'

Mitalee did not blink. 'You know where the squirrel is. Hand him over.'

Chintu held up an arm, as if shielding himself from Mitalee's gaze. 'Your eyes!' he snapped. 'You a witch

or something? You go find the squirrel. Why would I kidnap it?'

Mitalee's eyes turned larger still. 'Because you've tried before. That's how I know it's you. Hand him over!'

'Huh! Think you're always right, don't you? Watch, I'll prove you wrong. Stop staring and I'll prove to you that I don't have the squirrel.'

Mitalee blinked, restoring her eyes to their regular size.

'Witch eyes,' whispered Chintu, shaking his head. 'So, you believe I have your beloved white-headed squirrel? Totally convinced and all. Well, then, go find it. There, the door of my house is open. Go inside—go in and search. Check *every* room. And here's a promise from me: I swear that if you find it inside I will never shoot at birds or squirrels ever in my life! My buddies here are witnesses to this. They too will promise not to shoot at birds ever if you find the squirrel in there—isn't that right, guys?'

Arjun's face turned solemn. 'I swear on my mom and my dad and my baby brother that I will never shoot at any creature again if the bird girl's precious squirrel is in Chintu's house!'

Maitreya remained silent.

Mitalee opened her mouth to reply, but couldn't. She was at a loss for words. This had never happened before. Chintu inviting her to his house? Was she hearing right? In all the years she had had him as a neighbour, she had never crossed his threshold.

Chintu was grinning, enjoying her confusion. 'Go on, bird girl. The house is yours to search. We'll wait outside.'

Mitalee's mind raced. There was no way Snowdrop was inside. It was only because the squirrel wasn't in there that he was inviting her into his house and pledging to give up his catapult too—both offers thoroughly out of character for a bully like Chintu.

She spoke sharply. 'Don't take me for an idiot, Chintu. It's obvious that the squirrel is not in your house. I'm not as dumb as your stupid friends here. Even these halfwits would see through your posing and understand that the squirrel isn't hidden in there. But don't for a moment think that this great show of yours has fooled me into believing you have nothing to do with the squirrel's disappearance. I know it's *you* who is behind this! I will find the white-headed squirrel—be sure I will. And if any harm befalls him, you had better watch out. You will regret it so much that you'll wish you hadn't even been born!'

Chintu opened his mouth to retort, but Mitalee had already turned away. Striding to the wall, she pulled herself over and dropped into her garden. Moments later, there was a loud thud as she slammed her door shut behind her.

Mysun Remembers

Evenings at the Rose Garden were never like this. The gathering of birds at the fountain was always joyful— a time of high spirts, of play and jest. But that evening, as Mitalee watched from her room, their flocking was anything but happy.

The birds were present—perched on the fountain— but there was no fluttering, no frolicking, no merrymaking. They sat quietly, heads down, not a cheep or squawk escaping their beaks. So still were they that Mitalee felt she was staring at a huddle of birds at a funeral. It was only when the sun sank and shadows swept the garden that Mitalee finally heard some chatter.

A mournful sound, not very different from the whining of a dog, warbled from the fountain. Was it the magpie-robin? wondered Mitalee. The black-and-

white bird was Snowdrop's constant companion. Was he crying, grieving the loss of his friend?

It *was* the robin. The sorrowful sound was indeed trilling from his beak. The robin dropped to the lower ledge of the fountain, where the other birds—the bulbul, the black drongo, the yellow iora and the little sunbird—were perched.

Then the bulbul's beak started to move. For Mitalee the sound was nothing more than chirping. But for the birds assembled there, every cheep, chirrup and twitter made perfect sense.

'Stop crying, will you, Blackpie?' squawked Kabul the bulbul. Her tone was strict, as if she were scolding a child. Her head was turned to the magpie-robin, the bird that had been weeping like a hatchling. 'This isn't the time for weakness. Your best friend, Shikar, would never behave like this! If it were the other way round and *you* were missing, he would be scurrying everywhere and searching for you instead of crying. So stop this moaning and help us.'

'H-he was my b-best friend.' Blackpie sniffled. 'The only squirrel in the whole wide world who could speak

our language. So precious, so loving. None of you understand!'

Kabul exhaled loudly. To Mitalee, the sound was like a whistle.

'Stop it, Blackpie!' hooted the bulbul. 'You are a proud robin, not a whining lapwing. And Shikar *wasn't* your best friend—get that into your bird-brain. He *is* your best friend. He is alive and fine. Look, squirrels don't have wings. He can't fly far away like a bird and just disappear. He's here, somewhere nearby. Get a hold of yourself. Snap your feathers together and help us find him.'

Kabul hopped to the upper ledge of the fountain. She glowered at Blackpie before turning to the other birds. 'It's pointless slouching about like a flock of sulking herons,' she squawked. 'Our beloved Shikar disappeared yesterday morning. I want to know who saw him last, and where. Come on! Each of you! Put your bird-brains to work. Waggle them like you would your wings. *Where did you see him last?* Blackpie, you first. You're the one who's closest to Shikar. Tell us.'

Blackpie stared at his reflection in the fountain waters, thinking. Then he spoke. 'It was late when I left

the garden yesterday—well after sunrise. I flew with Bongo.'

'That's right,' chirped Bongo, the drongo, nodding his dark head. 'We flew together to the wires. We spent the day there, chatting with the other birds.'

'Excellent,' said Kabul. 'We've made a start. You said you left late, Blackpie. You must have been with Shikar. When and where did you last see him?'

'Shikar and I played together,' said Blackpie. 'We harassed Wow-Wow the dog—got him so angry that he barked the house down and the humans locked him away. It was so much fun . . .' The magpie-robin's eyes sparkled as he remembered the scene. 'Later, the doves Lovey and Dovey dropped by. They chatted with us. Shikar didn't want to play any more after they flew away. He told me he wanted to meet his squirrel friends in the Leaf Garden. That's when I flew away with Bongo. The last I saw of Shikar was him crossing over to the Leaf Garden.'

Senora, the iora, fluttered her wings. 'That reminds me,' she said. 'Whatever happened to Shikar's squirrel friends? I heard that horrible squealing after the humans attacked us. It was one of them, wasn't it?'

Kabul nodded. 'That was Supari. One of the humans struck her with a stone.'

'That's the girl squirrel, isn't it?' chirped the yellow bird. 'The one that's his girlfriend.'

'Let's not call her that. Shikar wouldn't like it—he's touchy about this. Anyway, yes, Supari was injured. Poor thing . . . But she's okay. Her brother, Paan, helped her and they both made it safely to the trees. I've checked on them—they are with their mother now.'

Kabul was a modest bird. She remained silent on her role in saving the squirrels, making no mention of the fearless attack she had launched on the humans.

'Hey!' squawked Senora. 'If Shikar went to play with the squirrels, they must surely know what's become of him. Why don't we—' But she broke off.

'You got it,' said Kabul. 'The language problem. None of us can speak Squirreleese. Shikar can, of course, but not us. Whatever they know, they can't tell us. But it's obvious that they too have no idea. They wouldn't have joined us this morning if they knew where Shikar was.'

'That's true,' said Senora. 'The squirrels don't know. I am no better than them, Kabul. There's nothing to report at my end. I wished Shikar goodbye about the time he was with the doves and Blackpie. Then I spent

the day on the far side of Lake Neelpaani, where the feeding for us ioras is good. I returned only at sunset, by which time we knew he was missing.'

'How about you, Bongo?' Kabul turned to the black drongo. 'When did you last see Shikar?'

'My account is the same as Blackpie's. We wished Shikar goodbye together when we left for the wires. He was crossing to the Leaf Garden then.'

'That leaves Mysun,' said Kabul, turning to the sunbird. 'What about you, Mysun? When did you see Shikar last?'

'Eh?' said Mysun. The sunbird hadn't been paying attention. He had been gazing at a nearby rose bush, dreaming of the delicious nectar stored there. Mysun peered at the bulbul. 'You talking to me?'

Kabul spoke patiently. 'Yes, Mysun, I am talking to you. When did you see Shikar last?'

The sunbird stared at Kabul, a confused look on his face.

'We're talking about *Shikar*, Mysun. *When did you last see him yesterday?*'

The sunbird clicked his long, curved beak. 'Shikar . . . yesterday,' he muttered. Then the feathers on his brow uncurled. 'Why . . . didn't we search for him this morning? I came along, remember?'

Blackpie flapped a wing. 'Hang on, Kabul,' he said. 'Let me handle this. Our sunbird friend hasn't been paying attention.' The magpie-robin hopped to where the sunbird was perched. 'You were dreaming—right, Mysun? I'm sure it was flowers. Tell me, which flowers were you dreaming of?'

The sunbird's eyes lit up. 'Roses,' he twittered.

'Roses,' clucked Blackpie. 'Wow. They are gorgeous, aren't they? Tell me, are they blooming today?'

The sunbird nodded excitedly. 'Three of them. Their fragrance—oh, you should smell them! And their nectar . . . mmm . . . it's beak-smacking good. So fresh, so pure, as if delivered from the skies—the kind that Greatbill would surely love.'

'Greatbill, huh? Wow! That good!' Blackpie whistled. 'But what about yesterday? Were the roses blooming yesterday too?'

Mysun shook his head. 'No. Yesterday it was the hibiscus.'

'Hibiscus? We don't have any hibiscus flowers here in the Rose Garden.'

'That's right,' said Mysun. 'Not here, but over in the Leaf Garden.'

'So I take it you were in the Leaf Garden yesterday.'

'Yes,' nodded Mysun, his beak widening in a smile. 'The whole day. The feeding was so good. But you know hibiscus nectar can't compare with rose. Nothing can.'

'That's right, Mysun. Rose is the best. But let's move on, hop away from nectar and flowers for a bit. Yesterday, while you were in the Leaf Garden, did you see Shikar there?'

The sunbird tucked his wings tight, thinking. 'Yes, now that you mention it, Shikar was there.'

Blackpie glanced at Kabul. The bulbul nodded. The other birds leaned forward.

'What was Shikar doing?' asked Blackpie.

Mysun looked puzzled. 'What was he doing? How should I know? He was there, that's all I know.'

'Do you remember what time you saw him?' asked the magpie-robin.

'The sun was high, I remember. That's when the flowers open fully. Shikar was there then . . . and yes, now I remember what he was doing. He was with this bird. You know the white bird, the one with the long tail feathers . . . the flycatcher?'

'Flycatcher with a long tail? Could it be a paradise flycatcher you're talking about?'

Mysun hopped up and down on the fountain ledge. 'Yes, that's the bird. I remember! It was a paradise flycatcher.'

'And then?' asked Blackpie. 'What happened next?'

'Next? Why, I went back to feeding on the hibiscus, of course.'

'What about Shikar?' asked Blackpie.

'How should I know?' said Mysun. 'He was minding his business, chatting with the paradise flycatcher, and I minded mine, lunching on hibiscus.'

Blackpie made to speak, but Kabul cut in. 'Did you see Shikar again after that, Mysun?'

The sunbird shook his head. 'Nope. Last I saw of him was with the paradise flycatcher. It was a very beautiful bird, I have to tell you. Almost as lovely as a flower.'

'Wow!' exclaimed Kabul. 'Coming from you, Mysun, comparison to a flower is high praise. That bird must truly have been beautiful. Thanks, Mysun. You've been super today! Your information on Shikar is great, better than all that the others have shared.'

Mysun puffed out his chest. He preened, fluffing his feathers. 'I'm intelligent. I know that.'

Blackpie made a sniggering sound. Kabul spun around, staring sternly at the robin.

'And, yes, I remember one more thing,' chirped Mysun. 'The paradise flycatcher was going on about hornbills, saying that they are his friends. He spoke a *lot* about hornbills. See, I'm intelligent because I remembered that too. I remembered because my beak is like a hornbill's—all curved and sharp!'

'Really?' said Blackpie. The magpie-robin stared at Mysun's slender, curved bill. 'Hmm . . . yes, your beak *is* shaped like a hornbill's. And it's as big and strong as a hornbill's too, right?'

Mysun gazed at Blackpie, confused.

Kabul squawked sharply, 'That's enough, Blackpie. Off with you now! You can return to your roost. You too, Mysun. The sun has set and the night is upon us. Flap your wings . . . Leave us now. Bongo, you and Senora stay back.'

From her window, Mitalee saw the sunbird and the magpie-robin fly away.

'I have some work for you tomorrow, Bongo,' said Kabul after the birds had gone.

'I know what you're thinking, Kabul,' said the drongo. 'So obvious. As clear to me as the sun in a blue sky. You want me to inquire about the paradise flycatcher at the wires, right?'

'That's right,' nodded the bulbul. 'And Senora, you will accompany Bongo. But don't just *ask* about the flycatcher. Find out where he is and track him down. The bird is our only lead. It's not much of a lead, a feathery one at best, but it's all we have to go on. Maybe the paradise bird has valuable information on Shikar—' Kabul clamped her beak shut, stifling a yawn. 'And I'll be doing some searching too. Blackpie will be helping me. We'll check all the gardens and scan the area around the lake. But it's late now. Time to sleep. Safe night, both of you. May Greatbill watch over you. We'll meet tomorrow.'

The black drongo melted into the night. The bulbul too vanished into the gloom.

But Mitalee, who was still watching from her window, tracked the iora, tracing the flash of the bird's yellow wings to the jacaranda tree, where she roosted every night.

Sahyadri School

'A squirrel,' muttered Mr Paranjpe, squinting at Mitalee's notebook.

A sketch of a squirrel smiled up at him from the open book. Although it was a fine portrait—the squirrel's eyes and furry face outlined with loving detail—Mr Paranjpe was in no mood to appreciate Mitalee's sketching skills. Slowly, and with great deliberation, he transferred his gaze from the notebook to Mitalee, staring at her through his thick owlish spectacles. 'So this is what you have been doing in class. Here I am, pouring all my energies into teaching you geography, yet you ignore me. My efforts mean nothing to you—you prefer to sketch instead. I find this disrespectful. Deeply disrespectful.'

Mr Paranjpe directed his gaze at Mitalee's notebook again and licked his index finger. Then, using the wet finger, he flicked through the pages of the book. The

same squirrel stared up at him from each page. Sighing, Mr Paranjpe turned to the students of his class. 'Here,' he said, waving Mitalee's notebook. 'See what your classmate has been doing. Drawing squirrels while I teach geography!'

The class waited. The students sat still, not moving. Mr Paranjpe's melon-shaped face was turning red— always a bad sign. He was a proud and pompous man. It was his firm belief that he was a person of great wisdom and that his instruction was of the highest quality. In his opinion, there could be no greater sin than daydreaming or distracting oneself in his class. Sketching squirrels while he was teaching was bound to draw his wrath. The situation did not bode well for Mitalee.

'I am a hard-working teacher,' said Mr Paranjpe. 'Far more dutiful than the other teachers of this school. I take great trouble preparing for class. The very least I can expect from my students is that they respect my efforts and pay attention. But not this girl. My toil, my exertions, they mean nothing to her.' Mr Paranjpe snorted loudly. 'Sketching! Unacceptable! I shall punish her. But I am a just human being. All of you know that. There is no one in this school who is as fair and high-minded as me. Maybe this girl was paying attention—it's possible. I will give her a chance to defend herself.'

Mr Paranjpe turned to Mitalee, smirking as he twirled his moustache. Mitalee was reminded of a cat. A smug cat that had cornered a bird and was toying with its whiskers before pouncing.

'Young lady, we have been talking about rivers. Important rivers that flow through the different continents of the world. I shall ask you a few questions— simple ones—simple, that is, for anyone who has been paying attention. I will select three continents. For each, I want you to name a river, just one river that flows there. Let's start with Africa. Name a river that flows in Africa.'

A hush fell upon the classroom. No one spoke. No one moved. Outside, a koel sang its lilting tune. Mitalee stood with her head down, staring at the ground. Mr Paranjpe twirled his moustache furiously, a catlike smile hovering on his lips.

'SIR!' A hand shot up from amidst the rows of desks. It was Maitreya, the boy who had injured the squirrel in Chintu's Leaf Garden. 'Sir, for Africa, the Nile is the most important river. It is the longest river in the world. Also, the Nile is one of the few rivers that flow from the south to the north, and for most of its journey, it travels through the desert of Egypt, allowing people to live in a land where there is hardly any water.'

The smile vanished from Mr Paranjpe's lips. His large eyes shrank behind his spectacles. 'Stupid boy,' he frothed, his tone clearly conveying that he was unimpressed with Maitreya's scholarly knowledge. 'Can

you not understand English? Is your name Mitalee? Did I ask *you* to answer the question?'

'No, sir,' replied the boy.

Mr Paranjpe banged his hand on his table so loudly that Mitalee jumped. Beads of spittle erupted from his mouth as he shouted, 'Then remain SILENT! Zip your mouth! Keep it shut or it is *you* I will punish and not the girl.' Mr Paranjpe stood breathing heavily for a while, his owlish spectacles sweeping the class. The children sensibly kept their heads down, not daring to look at him. Expelling his breath in a loud snort, he turned back to Mitalee. 'Name a river in South America.'

Maitreya's hand shot up again. 'Sir, the Amazon. It is one of the greatest rivers in the world. Its source is in the Andes Mountains and it flows mainly through Brazil. The forests that surround the river are among the finest in the world.'

This time spittle spouted Amazon-like from Mr Paranjpe. Mitalee hurriedly stepped aside as it squirted in a wet arc about her.

'AGAIN!' he howled. The class turned deadly quiet. Mr Paranjpe looked positively scary. His eyes had turned an ominous shade of red, their glow magnified by his spectacles. Spittle soaked the lower half of his face.

'Again you disobey me! How dare you! I warned you. Now it is *you* I shall punish. You will stay back in class every day. Every day, you hear me! Every day for the rest of the term. And you will work while you sit. You will write "I shall never disobey Mr Paranjpe again." You will fill an entire notebook each day and leave only after handing me the notebook. Is that understood?'

Maitreya nodded. 'Yes, sir.'

'Back,' he shouted at Mitalee. 'Get back and sit down.'

Thrilled at her let-off, Mitalee hurried to her seat, worried that Mr Paranjpe might change his mind and call her back. But the teacher switched his attention to the blackboard, resuming his lecture on the rivers of the world.

As Mr Paranjpe droned on, Maitreya's classmates sneaked glances at him, some marvelling at his pluck for taking on Mr Paranjpe, others wondering how he would cope with the heavy punishment doled out to him. But Maitreya seemed unruffled, as if his tiff with Mr Paranjpe was an ordinary occurrence. He smiled at the curious faces turned to him, winking at Chintu and Arjun when they looked at him. After a while, interest waned and his classmates stared dully at Mr Paranjpe as he strove to enlighten them about the Danube, the Volga and other great rivers.

While Mr Paranjpe lectured them about the Brahmaputra, tracing its turbulent flow across the Tibetan Plateau, Maitreya scribbled a note on a scrap of paper. Folding it, he handed it to Alisha, the girl sitting beside him. When she looked inquiringly at him, he pointed at Mitalee, who sat beside her. Shrugging, Alisha handed the note to Mitalee.

Mitalee slowly unfolded the note. Pointing at a map, Mr Paranjpe identified the sharp bend that the River Brahmaputra carves through the Himalayan Mountains to enter India. She stared at the scribbled message.

Deeply sorry for having injured the squirrel at Chintu's place. Promise never to do anything so cruel ever again.

Although Mitalee was keenly aware that Maitreya was staring at her, she did not look up. With no change of expression, she tore up the note and then gazed at Mr Paranjpe, who was now outlining the flow of the mighty river through the states of Arunachal and Assam.

The lunch bell rang when Mr Paranjpe was speaking about the River Ganges. The class quickly dispersed and outside, in the school quadrangle, Chintu and Arjun caught up with Maitreya.

'You crazy?' asked Arjun. 'Nobody ever takes on old Pompous the way you did!'

'I've never seen Pompous froth like that,' said Chintu. 'Whatever did you do that for? You got a crush on that bird girl, or what?'

'Nah,' said Maitreya. 'No crush. I was feeling bad for her. I saw her draw picture after picture of that squirrel. Poor thing. She really loves that squirrel, doesn't she?'

Chintu rolled his eyes. 'Aw . . . poor thing,' he said with great drama. 'Poor, poor thing.'

Arjun grinned. 'Yeah. Poor thing! I pity her, because she's never going to find her beloved pet.'

'Ha ha ha!' laughed the two boys.

'Hey,' said Maitreya, 'why do you say she's never going to find the squirrel? And what's so funny? Do you guys know something about this?'

'Nah!' Chintu waved dismissively. 'How would we know? We just don't like pets, that's all. Not exotic pets like squirrels, right, Arjun?'

'Nope, we don't like pets,' said Arjun. 'No to pets. No to pet exotica.'

Chintu's face lit up. '*No to pet exotica!*' Then he erupted with laughter again.

Maitreya stared at his friends. They were beside themselves with laughter. 'Pet exotica?' he queried. 'What's this pet exotica business? I don't understand.'

Chintu wiped tears from his eyes. 'It's okay,' he said, fighting to control his mirth. 'Forget about it. Just a joke between Arjun and me.'

'Yeah,' said Arjun, 'forget about it. We've got to go. It's late. We won't find seats in the dining hall.'

Chintu placed an arm around Maitreya's shoulder as they walked. 'Some advice for you, Maitreya. You're new around here, but don't do what you just did again.

Don't stick your neck out again in old Pompous's class, especially not for that bird girl and her squirrel.'

'Hey,' said Arjun. 'Speaking of the bird girl, there she is.'

Maitreya looked up. Mitalee and Alisha were stepping out of the dining hall. Their eyes met and Maitreya's heart leapt. Mitalee's gaze wasn't cold, as it had been on the earlier occasions they had crossed each other.

Was there a glimmer of warmth in them? But Maitreya was destined never to know because at that moment, Mitalee saw Chintu—and his arm around Maitreya's shoulder. Her eyes flickered, frosting over, and she looked away.

'Oh, my,' sneered Chintu, spotting Mitalee abruptly turning her head. 'Looking away. Snobbish, aren't we?'

'Don't be mean, Chintu,' said Arjun. 'Can't you see? She's missing her dear white-headed squirrel.'

'Oh, yes, her pet. Her favourite pet, the squirrel. Hah. He's gone. Gone forever. Poor squirrel, sad squirrel.'

'Pet exotica!' said Arjun.

Both burst out laughing. Mitalee and Alisha swept by, paying no heed to the cackling. The boys entered the dining hall, Chintu and Arjun still sniggering.

The Wires

The wires are a hang-out for birds. So popular are they that every area has its own wires, where local birds gather to swap stories and trade gossip. The wires in Neelpaani were a set of human telephone lines strung through an open field, just a short flight from the Rose Garden. Birds thronged the wires every day. Most stopped to chat and exchange news before flying on. But there were those that chose to spend their entire day there. These were the regulars, and every set of wires had its enthusiasts— who, come rain or shine, always visited, never missing a day. For many summers now, Neelpaani's regulars were Bongo the drongo and his friends—Ming, the kingfisher, and Stroller, the roller.

Bongo's friends were already perched on the wires when he and Senora flew in the next morning.

'There you are, Bongo,' greeted Stroller the roller. 'Late as usual. We can always count on our black-feathered friend being the last to arrive.'

'Yeah,' chirped Ming the kingfisher. 'Not like us. We are the early birds. We get the worms. You don't, Bongo! Ha ha!'

Stroller snorted. 'Bad joke,' he said. 'Stupid. Like something humans might chirp. Hey, who's this birdie with Bongo? An iora, I see. Who's your iora friend, Bongo?'

Bongo introduced Senora.

'Hey,' squawked Ming, 'we heard about your Rose Garden squirrel. The white-headed one. He's missing, right?'

Senora was surprised. 'How did you birds get to know?' she asked.

'News streaks across the wires,' boasted the kingfisher. 'Flashes faster than even a peregrine falcon. We know everything.'

'Yeah,' squawked Stroller. 'This is the place you come to for news. Everything you want to know about our bird world, you'll learn here. It's true! I'm a dumb dodo if what I say is false. Even news of penguins— perched here on these wires, we know what's happening in their distant ice-bound home. And migrations?

We have the latest on them. Up-to-date accounts, that's what we'll give you. The Arctic terns, the cranes, the godwits, the seagulls—you can learn about all those epic journeys across the planet here. Bird-nappings, the weather, gossip, matters of the Sky Council—the latest, the trending stories—that's what we broadcast here at the wires. *This* is the place to be.'

Ming bobbed his head. 'Yeah, it's all happening here. But tell us about your squirrel. Is he dead? Did a kill-bird get him?'

'No, he isn't dead,' said Senora. 'He's missing! He was last seen the day before with a paradise flycatcher. I've come here for news on the flycatcher. Has any bird seen one lately in Neelpaani?'

'A paradise flycatcher?' Stroller frowned. 'No, not that I know of. None have dropped by the wires recently.'

'That's what I thought,' said Bongo. 'But there could be some in the area. We have to find out. This is a job for the scouts. Call them in, Ming. Sound the call!'

Ming puffed out his chest and trumpeted a loud, piercing call. Filling his chest once more, he boomed another, this one even louder.

Almost instantly, a bird call echoed in reply.

Stroller nodded appreciatively. 'Excellent scouts, these minivets. Young and raw they may be, but they seem mighty capable. The Sky Council should be told about them.'

'Uh-uh,' said Bongo. 'Not yet. It's too early to take a call on them. Yes, they are good birds, but they have to prove themselves. We'll test them with the paradise flycatcher. Let's see if they find the bird.'

It wasn't long before two birds flew in. Both were brightly coloured: one red and the other a dazzling yellow. Senora was introduced to the birds. The red minivet—male—was Scarlet and the yellow one— female—was Bright-Jet.

Bongo quickly described the nature of the assignment to the birds. 'Search the area fast,' said the drongo in conclusion. 'Find the paradise flycatcher. There's no time to be lost. Fly away now. May Greatbill speed your wings.'

'Can I go with them?' asked Senora. 'I could help.'

The minivets looked at each other. They shuffled awkwardly and fluffed their wings.

'You'll slow them down,' said Stroller. 'Scarlet and Bright-Jet are trained scouts. They work as a team. Leave this task to them.'

'Sorry,' squawked Scarlet as he rose, flapping his crimson wings.

'Another time!' Bright-Jet smiled. Her wings blazed gaudily as she followed Scarlet to the sky.

Time passed quickly on the wires. Afterwards, Senora wouldn't recall a single dull moment during the hours she spent waiting for the minivets to return. Birds kept dropping by, delivering news from far and wide. Senora discovered that the monsoon winds had started to blow early. A sandpiper had noticed their blustery presence on a pebbly beach. The sandpiper had told an egret, who'd told a parakeet, who'd told the green barbet that dropped by on the wires. The iora also found out that the summer heat had turned intense; ponds were

drying up and water was turning scarce
in the forests. A hoopoe broadcasted
the water story. A sulking heron, for
whom the ponds were a source
of food, confirmed the
hoopoe's story. The
wires were a

place of learning too. Senora learnt
about geese and cranes and their
migration, about the hornbills
of the Southern Forests* and
about partridges that lived in
the cold, snowy mountains.

* The expanse of the forests of Wayanad, Mudumalai, Bandipur and
Nagarhole in southern India.

Very soon, Bongo's devotion to the wires became clear to Senora. She now understood why he never missed a single day here. The wires suited the black bird's personality perfectly. If there was any such thing as a bird of leisure, then it was Bongo who embodied that role. The drongo hated hard work and exercise. His favourite pastime was talk and gossip. The wires were just the place for him, as the only exertion here was the waggling of beaks. His friends Ming the kingfisher and Stroller the roller were no different from Bongo. They delighted in the constant movement of birds and in the exchange of news and gossip and rumour and scandal.

The minivets returned around noon, when the sun was high and the heat so strong that it fogged the air, causing the trees and grasses to seem all bent and misshapen.

The scout birds delivered good news and bad. The good news was that a paradise flycatcher *had* passed through the lake area recently. The bad news was that the flycatcher had moved on, flying back to his home in the Southern Forests.

The scout minivets were certain that the paradise flycatcher was the one that had visited the gardens. They were eager to track him down and question him about Shikar and his disappearance.

'I'll come with you,' volunteered Senora. 'The forests are huge, everyone says. Tracking a bird amidst all those trees won't be easy.'

'That's true,' said Scarlet. 'The forest *is* big.'

'You can come along,' said Bright-Jet. 'Your help will be welcome on this mission. How about you, Bongo? Would you like to join us? We could use additional wings.'

Bongo made a rasping sound, like he was clearing his throat. 'Um . . . I'm not feeling up to it. Had a cold yesterday. You know . . . the kind that leaves you all weak and tired. You carry on, minivets, and take Senora with you. I'll only slow you down.'

Ming and Stroller exchanged glances.

'Fly on then,' said Bongo. 'There's no time to waste. Bring back news of our squirrel friend. Hurry! May Greatbill shower blessings and luck upon you.'

So the minivets and Senora flew away, speeding south to the forests.

Friends

Maitreya's family was new to the gardens. It had been just two months since his father had secured a job at the Neelpaani Dam. Senior engineers at the dam were provided homes in the gardens, and the one allotted to Maitreya's family was called Marigold.

It was late and the Marigold Garden was shrouded in shadow. Maitreya's room on the upper floor of the Marigold Bungalow was dark too. It was past his bedtime. His mother had entered a short while earlier and, after tucking him in bed, turned off the lights.

Sleep, however, was the last thing on Maitreya's mind. He had other plans. The murmur of the TV drifted up from the hall downstairs. His parents had switched on the news. They always did so before retiring for the night. Except for the TV, there was no other sound.

It was time.

Maitreya stirred. Rising, he reached under his blanket. His fingers retrieved the phone and the iPad he had hidden there. Fumbling, he switched on the phone. When the dial pad lit up, he tapped out Alisha's number.

'Hi,' greeted Maitreya when the call was answered.

Alisha's voice was guarded. 'Hi, Maitreya,' she replied.

'I need to talk to Mitalee.'

'Really, Maitreya. Mitalee has always said that you lack intelligence. I didn't believe her, but obviously I was wrong. You do know that Mitalee would rather chat with a dragon than with you, right?'

'Look, I know she doesn't like me, but this is urgent. Tell her it's about the white-headed squirrel.'

Alisha's tone sharpened. 'The white-headed squirrel? What do you know about the squirrel? Are *you* the one who's kidnapped him?'

'Don't be silly. I have nothing to do with his disappearance. I have information instead. Important information. And no, I'm not joking, nor am I lying. Tell her to call me. Actually, it's best if she chats with me on Facebook.'

Alisha tittered. 'Facebook! You have this habit of making impossible demands, you know. Wonder what you'll want from her next. That she gives you a thousand likes on Facebook? Or even better, that she becomes your devoted follower on Instagram and sings your praises on the Net. You're living in a dreamworld, Maitreya. Get this: Mitalee will *never* friend you on Facebook. That's your first reality check. And if by some miracle she does, you should know that her parents are even worse than the police when it comes to the Internet. Weekdays, she is barred from using the Internet, and at this late hour, you can totally forget it.'

'You don't understand, Alisha. This is important. Important like you can't believe! Tell her to hide from her parents. She must come online now—*right now*. There's stuff here that she has to see. And no, I don't have a habit of making impossible demands . . . this is an emergency. Trust me. Tell Mitalee I've sent her a friend request already. She must accept. I'm online now and waiting. Please don't argue, Alisha. I'll buy you as many ice creams as you want—a year's supply at the school canteen! It's a promise!'

Alisha had half a mind to hang up the phone. But there was a ring of sincerity in Maitreya's voice that she found hard to ignore. Whatever Mitalee might say, Alisha liked the boy. She might even have been his friend if it weren't for Mitalee's obvious loathing for him.

Alisha swallowed her misgivings. 'Okay,' she said. 'It's a year's supply of ice cream—I'll hold you to it. I'll call Mitalee and she'll come online in a bit; I'll persuade her. This had better be important because if it isn't, I'm going to take that canteen ice cream and stuff it down the back of your shirt every day.' She disconnected the phone before Maitreya could thank her.

Maitreya waited. It wasn't just Mitalee who would be breaking rules if she connected with him online. There would be trouble for Maitreya too if his parents caught him.

The room was dark except for the glow from the iPad. The TV rumbled on in the hall below. The minutes dragged by. A reporter was droning about the arrival of the monsoon when the iPad beeped. Maitreya's heart leapt—Mitalee had accepted his friend request! However, the message that flashed on his screen was anything but friendly.

Mitalee

If it is you who has kidnapped my Snowdrop, you are a dead man.

Maitreya pounded out his reply.

Maitreya

If it is me, you are welcome to knock me off. Strap weights to my legs, like they do in movies, and drop me into Lake Neelpaani.

The next message was to the point.

 Mitalee

Do you have any news on Snowdrop? If you don't, I'll sign off and delete you from my friend list.

Maitreya

Don't. Here it is. There's a link copied here for you. Click on it and have a look.

Maitreya opened the link himself while he waited. A photo of the white-headed squirrel popped up on his screen. Mitalee's response was swift.

RARE
WHITE-HEADED
SQUIRREL
FOR SALE!

Mitalee

SNOWDROP! This is my Snowdrop! Who has done this? Who are these wretched people?

Maitreya

I don't know, Mitalee. But Chintu and Arjun are involved. They know about this. This is the PetExotica website. Remember? They kept repeating the words 'pet' and 'exotica' and laughing? So I checked on the Internet.

 Mitalee

I'll get them arrested! Jail them. How dare they? Pigs. Porcupines!

Maitreya

Take it easy, Mitalee. You can't get them arrested. There is no proof they are involved.

 Mitalee

Proof! Can't you see? Snowdrop's photo is before your eyes. What more do you want?

Maitreya

PetExotica is not their website. I've checked.
There are loads of other animals for sale on
the site: zebras, hyenas, turtles. They even
have endangered ones. There are birds too. This
website is a big operation. Too big for wannabes
like Chintu and Arjun. Way out of their league.

Mitalee

Then who are they? How do we stop them? How
do I get my Snowdrop back?

Maitreya

I've studied the website, Mitalee. Searched it
thoroughly. There is no address on the site. The
only contact is a messaging facility. This is
a well-organized operation that only deals in
exotic animals. They would never sell anything
as common as a squirrel. But Snowdrop's white
head makes him exotic—it's unique and rare.
That's why they've put him up for sale.

Mitalee

My Snowdrop IS rare, he IS exotic. He is
the most wonderful squirrel in the whole
wide world. I want my squirrel back!

Maitreya

We'll get him back for you, Mitalee. But we have to do this carefully, intelligently. Now listen. The people who own the website don't have him. See, I responded to their photo of Snowdrop— I messaged them that I wanted to buy the squirrel. But I put down a condition: I said I wanted to see the squirrel before paying. They replied promptly. They said this wasn't possible. They don't keep the pets they sell. Only when they get the money do they collect the pet and deliver. I asked them where the squirrel was being kept. They replied that he was being held where he was captured—in Maharashtra, in the Western Ghats region. They refused to provide any further information. Pay up, they said, and they would deliver the squirrel to me.

Mitalee

I'll pay. I'll do anything to get Snowdrop back.

Maitreya

The price is Rs 5 lakhs. No discount, they said. He's the only white-headed squirrel in the world.

Mitalee

☹☺☹ Robbers! Dakoos! Cheats! I can't pay that much. My dad would go broke.

Maitreya's fingers hammered away on the iPad.

> **Maitreya**
>
> Exactly. So we can't buy him back. Here are the facts: Chintu and Arjun have captured Snowdrop. They are holding him somewhere. He isn't at Chintu's house, neither is he at Arjun's. I've been to both their homes, so I know. They are keeping him somewhere here in Neelpaani. I'm sure about this. Also, these past few days I've been hearing Chintu and Arjun talk of things they plan to buy. Gadgets, like the latest mobiles, iPads, Xboxes, skateboards, even imported cycles. First I thought they were just bragging to impress me, but now, after seeing the website and Snowdrop's price tag, their big talk is making sense. !!!!! Hang on . . . my mom's coming! Stay online—we'll continue after she leaves.

Maitreya had heard footsteps. Moving fast, he locked his iPad and tucked it under his pillow. He collapsed in bed just as the door opened. The footsteps padded to his bedside. Maitreya kept his eyes shut. He sensed a shadow lean over him. He smelled his mother's perfume as her lips brushed his cheek. Then the footsteps receded and the door was shut gently.

Maitreya waited a few minutes before switching on his iPad.

Maitreya

That was close! Just managed by pretending to be asleep when Mom came in.

 Mitalee

It is late. My mom should be coming up any minute too. She'll be hopping mad if she catches me . . . I'll be grounded for sure.

Maitreya

Okay. We'll meet and make a plan tomorrow.

 Mitalee

Yes. And thanks, Maitreya. I was wrong about you.

Maitreya

I made mistakes.

Mitalee

Choosing the wrong friends for starters.

Maitreya

That I did.

 Mitalee

And injuring a squirrel.

Maitreya

Don't remind me. That was the most shameful deed of my life. Still haunts me.

 Mitalee

It should. It was a terrible thing you did.

Maitreya

Sorry. I won't ever shoot at an animal again. That's a promise. A promise from the deepest place in my heart.

 Mitalee

That's very sweet of you, Maitreya. Don't worry, I forgive you. I take back all the horrible things I said about you. ☺

Maitreya

Thanks. ☺

 Mitalee

I should have listened to Alisha. She said you were a nice guy.

Maitreya

☺

 Mitalee

We're friends now.

Maitreya

Friends. ☺

The Paradise Flycatcher

A necessary talent for selection as a scout bird is the ability to fly fast. Senora quickly discovered that her minivet companions were energetic and speedy flyers. The iora had to beat her wings furiously to keep up with them. The birds streaked across the skies, winging over fields, mountains, valleys, rivers and human staans.[*] The Southern Forests were far and the sky had started to darken, when a magnificent forest, hilly and packed with trees, unfurled beneath them. Folding their wings, they dropped to the canopy, touching down on a tall tree with thick, twisted branches.

Night was falling. It was far too late to search for the paradise flycatcher. Also, the birds were hungry and tired. Fortunately, they were in a forest. There were trees everywhere, many laden with fruits and berries

---

[*] Cities, where humans live.

and nuts. Senora and the minivets pecked a quick meal and settled in for the night.

Loud birdsong roused them at dawn. Birds were raucously welcoming the new day, crooning and singing and calling to one another. The noisiest was a black bird with a long fanlike tail, perched high on a nearby tree.

'Hmm,' said Bright-Jet, looking up. 'That drongo bird sure has a loud voice.'

Senora looked up too. 'That's not a drongo,' she said.

'Uh-huh,' said Bright-Jet. 'That *is* a drongo.'

'But he's much bigger than our Bongo. His tail too. Look, it's longer and different.'

'Uh-huh,' said Scarlet. 'Bright-Jet is right. That bird is a drongo. But he's not the kind our dear Bongo is. This one's a racket-tailed drongo. Wait here, both of you. I'll ask for directions to the local wires.'

Scarlet winged to the top of the tree and perched beside the racket-tailed drongo. Like Bongo, this drongo was black all over. But the bird was larger. He had a prominent crest on his head and his tail was ornamented with big leaf-shaped feathers.

After a lengthy chat, Scarlet returned and hovered before his friends. 'Let's go, birdies,' he said, flashing his

bright red feathers. 'Time to work our wings again. The forest wires aren't far, according to the drongo. He says the wires are the best place to inquire. Also, the local scout birds are nice and helpful.'

The birds took to their wings. They broke through the tree cover and flew high in the sunlit sky. Senora marvelled at the forest below as she tailed the minivets. Trees covered the entire area, stretching as far as the eye could see.

The wires weren't easy to find. Senora was certain she would never have found them on her own. But the minivets were experienced scout birds. Even with no landmarks to guide them, they sped above the forest and dived into the canopy exactly where the wires were located.

'Wow!' exclaimed Senora when she broke through the tree cover and spotted the wires. 'How did you know they were here?'

'No big deal,' said Scarlet. 'Human things are easy to find. You just need to keep your eyes open.'

'My eyes *were* open,' said Senora. 'Just like yours were. But I didn't see the wires. All I saw was forest!'

'Ah . . . yes. Well, there's more to it. You have to know humans and their ways too. You see, the forest is natural everywhere. Everything in Greatbill's world is natural, but what humans do is never so. In a forest, whatever they do stands out—easily visible like the gaudy colours of my wings. You can tell straight away.'

Senora frowned. 'So . . . what was it that you saw?'

'We saw exactly what you saw, Senora,' said Scarlet. 'No different. Only thing is that we could make sense of what we saw. We noticed that the trees here are all planted in a line—a straight line.'

'That's true,' said Senora, staring at the tangle of green about her.

'You can see that for yourself now. Bright-Jet and I observed the row of trees from above. They were so perfectly straight—like a column of baby ducks marching behind their mother. Now, if you fly over forests often, like Bright-Jet and I do, then you would know that there are no straight lines in a forest. Trees grow randomly in a forest. Not in any kind of formation and never ever in a line. So when you see trees all in a perfect row, you know it isn't natural. It isn't something created by the forest. It is humans who have done it. That's how we guessed the wires were here. You learn these things on duty as a scout bird.'

The forest wires here were identical to the ones back home, at the gardens. Their setting was different, of course—these were located in a thickly forested area while the garden ones were set amidst fields. But their framework was the same: a row of poles with wires stretched between them.

At this early hour, there were only two birds on the wires—one a leafbird, and the other an oriole.

Senora quickly explained their quest to the birds.

'Do you know the name of the paradise flycatcher?' asked the leafbird when Senora was done.

'No,' said Senora.

The leafbird stared. Then he turned to his friend next to him, the oriole. 'You hear that, Pole? They've flown all this distance to search for a bird, they say—a bird whose name they don't even know! Sounds like a hopeless quest to me. Imagine searching for a cuckoo's egg in a nest filled with other eggs. You can't do that if you don't even know what the cuckoo's egg looks like! Same problem here. How do you find a bird when you don't know their name? You want to do your homework before you start, don't you?'

Pole the oriole shook his beak. 'Crazy,' he said. 'These forests are home to hundreds of paradise flycatchers. Without a name, you're going to go loony, like howler monkeys! If your plan is to stop every flycatcher you come across and ask if he had visited your lake, it will take you forever and more.'

The minivets and the iora gazed at each other. They hadn't given any thought to how they would track down

the flycatcher. The enormity of their task now dawned on them.

The pretty leafbird, whose name was Emerald, took pity on the crestfallen birds. 'Look, we are scouts, Pole and I. We'll help. I've heard about this white-headed squirrel of yours at the wires. Birds that pass by talk about him. The only squirrel on Terra-staan* who speaks our language. We wouldn't want a special squirrel like him to disappear. We'll do our best.'

So the birds searched the forests. The hours passed quickly. Senora came across so many paradise flycatchers that she started to wonder if the birds were as common in the Southern Forests as crows were in a human staan. Although several among whom she interviewed had stopped by Neelpaani during their travels, none had visited the gardens.

It was evening by the time the iora returned to the wires. The scout birds were there already, having arrived earlier. Their experience had been the same as hers. Paradise flycatchers were everywhere in the forest but none they had met had visited the gardens.

Senora perched dejectedly on a wire, her wings drooping. Things weren't going well. Her mission could

---

* Planet Earth.

turn out to be a failure. Depressed, she only half-listened to the other birds as they chatted.

Bright-Jet had enjoyed her time in the forest. She chattered about the animals she had seen that day: bears, elephants, deer, wild boar, mighty gaurs, monkeys. 'This Southern Forest of yours is wonderful,' she told the leafbird and the oriole.

'Yeah,' said Emerald the leafbird. 'Humans don't bother us much. That's why our forest is so nice.'

'So many hornbills,' said Scarlet. 'I haven't seen such a flocking of hornbills ever. Our lake area has a few, but—'

'Hornbills!' squawked Senora. 'The paradise flycatcher is a friend of the hornbills! I remember now— that's what Mysun told us.'

Pole the oriole frowned. 'Friend of the hornbills, huh? You sure, birdie iora? Hornbills don't mix with other birds, least of all flycatchers. You have to be careful with hornbills. They can attack—and then snack on your remains.'

Senora ignored the comment about the alarming behaviour of the birds. She sprang from her wire and hovered before the other birds. 'Where do the hornbills gather? Do you know?'

'There are trees nearby where they flock—'

'Take us there,' begged Senora. 'One last effort for the day. Please?'

Pole shrugged his wings. 'Sure. No big deal. The trees aren't far—just a few mountains away. Come along.'

Pole was right, the hornbill roost was just a few wing-flaps from the wires. It was late evening when they came to a giant tree so crowded with hornbills that it was hard to see the branches they perched upon. The birds were large, they had a funny crest on their heads and their beaks were ridiculously long and curved.

'Let me handle this,' said Emerald. 'Keep your distance. Hornbills are mostly peaceful, but you can never tell.'

The birds hung back as Emerald flew to the hornbill tree and landed on the tip of a branch. The hornbills took no notice. Only the bird nearest to him turned her neck inquiringly.

'Um,' began Emerald, 'we are looking for a paradise flycatcher.'

'That's easy,' said the hornbill in a booming voice. 'Just fly about. They are everywhere. You'll surely find one.'

'It's not any paradise flycatcher we are searching for. We want the one that's just returned from Neelpaani, the blue lake north of here.'

The hornbill cocked her head. 'Hey, you're in luck, Mr Leafbird. We have a paradise flycatcher here who got back a couple of days ago. Neelpaani, you said? Our little feller returned from there.'

Senora streaked forward and hovered before the hornbill. 'Did this flycatcher say anything about an area called the gardens?'

'Yeah,' said the hornbill. 'Now that you speak of it, yes, the place was something to do with gardens. He even talked of a squirrel that speaks our language. Can you believe it? A squirrel that you can talk to? But that's history. He said that the squirrel got caught by humans—'

'Where? *Where?*' cried Senora. 'WHERE IS THIS FLYCATCHER?'

The iora screeched so loudly that she caused a flutter amongst the gathered hornbills. An angry murmur rippled through the birds. Many had been napping and were upset at having been disturbed.

'My!' said the hornbill. 'For a small bird, you have a loud voice, don't you? I should be swatting you for

speaking so rudely and bothering my mates. But I'll let that pass because the paradise flycatcher you speak of is a friend of ours. Look up—look at the top of the tree. What do you see there, little bird?'

Senora's tiny heart leapt. A great wave of joy surged through her sunshine feathers. Up, on top of the tree was the most beautiful bird she had ever seen. His head was dark, but the rest of his slender frame was a sparkling white—so bright and pure that it could be mistaken for the snow that capped the Impossible Mountains.* Her mission was accomplished. Shikar would be saved. They had found the missing paradise flycatcher.

* The Himalayas.

Bicycle Chase

'Yoo-hoo!' hailed Maitreya. 'Hi there.'

'Hey,' said Alisha, braking her bicycle to a halt. 'Good morning.'

It was the weekend. There was no school today, and the children were out on their bicycles. Maitreya had entered the dusty bazaar area of Neelpaani Town and spotting Alisha, had pedalled fast to catch up with her. It was a warm summer morning and, although it was still early in the day, the sun was baking the streets of Neelpaani.

'Something's up,' said Maitreya, halting his cycle alongside Alisha's.

She nodded. 'Seems to be.'

'What time did you reach Arjun's place?' asked Maitreya.

'First thing in the morning, about seven-ish. I heard his mom firing the milkman for bringing the milk in late.'

'That's about the time I arrived at Chintu's,' said Maitreya. 'I stopped at Mitalee's gate actually. Kept an eye on Chintu's place from there. Mitalee gave me company.'

Alisha glared at Maitreya. 'Told you, didn't I? Not to Facebook her at night.'

On the night Maitreya and Mitalee had been exchanging messages online, Mitalee's mother had entered her room just as she had been shutting down her tablet. Mitalee had been punished for breaking the rules—grounded for the weekend.

Maitreya hung his head. 'I feel terrible about it,' he sighed.

'Mitalee's lucky. She got off lightly this time. She's been punished worse before.' Alisha's gaze softened. 'There's a bright side to all this, isn't there? We are a team now. We'll track down these dirty squirrel-nappers and get Snowdrop back!'

The bonding of Maitreya and the girls was the heartening result of the late-night chat. The three had united behind the common cause of rescuing Snowdrop. At school, they had decided upon shadowing

Chintu's and Arjun's every move. Their reasoning was that if the boys had locked Snowdrop in a cage somewhere, they would have to feed him. There was every possibility then that pursuing the boys, watching their every movement, could lead them to Snowdrop. They had stalked the boys after school the previous evening, but nothing had come out of it. Since it was the weekend, they had resumed their tracking early, at sunrise. Maitreya had waited outside Chintu's gate and Alisha at Arjun's.

'Something's definitely up, I think,' said Maitreya as he gazed across the road at Chintu and Arjun. 'There must be a reason behind the two of them meeting here, at the bazaar. This could lead to something.'

Both Chintu and Arjun had emerged from their homes at about the same time—only minutes earlier. Each had mounted his cycle and biked to the bazaar, where they had met up. Maitreya and Alisha had followed. Maitreya had then spotted Alisha and the two of them had halted opposite the cycle shop.

'I'm glad we are together now,' said Alisha. 'That Arjun gives me the creeps.'

'Both are nasty,' said Maitreya. 'They've dumped me as a friend now that I've switched sides. They haven't been nice to me since.'

'Hey, squirrel lovers,' called out Arjun from across the road. 'Think you're smart, don't you? Track Arjun and Chintu 24/7. Follow, and they will lead you to the white-headed squirrel! Wow, that's clever thinking. Very clever—real Einsteins, both of you.'

'Heh-heh,' sneered Chintu, standing beside Arjun. 'Nutty as hell. Must be the nuts they eat like their squirrel friends do.'

Both boys roared with laughter. 'Nutty!' cried Chintu, clutching his sides.

'Maitreya is the nut behind this,' continued Arjun when their laughing subsided. 'He's the brainiest—sorry, *nuttiest*—kid in class. Well, we'll give you something to chew on, nut lovers. The last nut, the very last nut in your white-headed squirrel's coffin.'

'Yeah!' said Chintu. 'We win. You lose. Your white-headed squirrel will soon be gone forever. We're going to get rich. And all you will have are nuts in your pockets!'

A black van swept up the dusty road and stopped next to the boys. A door opened. The boys entered and slammed the door behind them.

'Follow!' shouted Maitreya, pedalling as the van started to move. Alisha sped her bike forward. The van quickly accelerated. Maitreya and Alisha pedalled furiously but, despite their best efforts, the van pulled away. Soon they were out of the bazaar area and the road broadened.

'Nutty dreams, squirrel lovers!' shouted Arjun as the van sped away.

Maitreya halted when the van was but a speck on the road. 'I-it's pointless,' he panted. 'We don't stand a chance on our bikes. They've got away.'

Alisha's eyes were filled with tears. 'We have to stop them! You heard them—they're getting their money. They're giving Snowdrop away! Poor Mitalee. She'll never be the same if she loses him.'

'I've memorized the van's number,' said Maitreya. 'Come on. Let's head to Mitalee's. We're not giving up.'

Alisha and Maitreya raced their cycles. It was several minutes before they made it to the Rose Garden.

Mitalee was at the gate, her face streaked with tears.

'S-S-Snowdrop,' she sobbed. 'They've sold him. The website says "SOLD" next to his photo. Oh, Alisha, Maitreya . . . my Snowdrop is gone.'

Shikar

'You sure this is the den?' asked Kabul the bulbul.

'This is it,' said Snow-prise, the paradise flycatcher. 'I tracked the human boys here. This is where they brought the white-headed squirrel.'

The human den below them was small, more a shed or a garage rather than an actual home. From the sky it looked even tinier than it was, as it was set in a huge yard with a scattering of trees and grass. A doo-doo* was parked in the yard and the door of the den was open.

The birds touched down on a flowering copper pod tree that grew beside the den. If a human birdwatcher had been looking on, he would have marvelled at the birds flocked in the tree. The most eye-catching of them

---

* The vehicle that humans travel in.

all—the bird of jaw-dropping beauty—was the paradise flycatcher. But equally delightful were the two minivets, one of them a dazzling shade of red and the other a bright yellow. There was another yellow bird too, the iora, and completing the flock were a bulbul and a magpie-robin.

Senora the iora was tired. Unlike the scout minivets' wings, which were accustomed to constant flying, hers weren't anywhere near as hardy or strong. The non-stop flight that morning had drained her.

They had departed the Southern Forests in the darkness, several hours before dawn. The birds had flown hard and fast—much faster than on the outward journey—and had arrived at the Rose Garden a short while earlier.

Kabul had been delighted to see Snow-prise and overjoyed to discover that the paradise flycatcher had witnessed Shikar's abduction. Snow-prise had explained that the only reason he had dropped by the gardens was to meet its famous bird-language-speaking squirrel. Snow-prise had been fascinated with Shikar and they had spent a considerable amount of time together. It was after their meeting, while Snow-prise was flitting amongst the trees, hunting for his lunch, that the squirrel-napping had taken place. Two boys had lured

the squirrel into a cage by placing some fruits inside it. After trapping him, they had mounted their bicycles and cycled far, to a human den—the very den in the yard below. Snow-prise had trailed them, flying above. He had seen them place the cage inside the den and then cycle away.

'I spotted a falcon in the sky soon after,' the flycatcher had said. 'He had seen me and was circling above. I'm terrified of falcons—one almost got me some time back. So I lay low, hiding in the trees. When he was gone, I flew away. Straight home to my forests. I'm sorry, my plan was to come to the Rose

Garden and report the squirrel-napping, but the falcon spoiled all that.' The paradise flycatcher had then led them to the yard.

Now, settled in the copper pod tree, Kabul stared at the human den, her heart aflutter. If the flycatcher's information was correct, her beloved squirrel was in there. She might soon be united with him. But first, she had to establish that Shikar was indeed there.

Kabul turned to the magpie-robin. 'Blackpie,' she said, 'drop down to that window below. Peep inside. Check if there are any humans about. Look for Shikar too. Our dear squirrel should be inside.'

Blackpie flew to the window. Barely had he settled there when the black-and-white bird took flight again, shooting back to the tree, squawking jubilantly, 'Shikar is here! He's inside, locked in a cage. My friend is alive! Oh, this is the greatest day ever . . . I am the happiest magpie-robin alive.'

There was an explosion of joyful screeching from the tree. The birds' happiness knew no bounds. Blackpie wheeled in the sky, Senora flapped an energetic jig and even the usually restrained Kabul bounced like a human baby. At last—at long, long last—they had found their dear lost friend.

Kabul cautioned the birds when the celebrations had died down. 'Rein in your wings,' she warned. 'Don't let them carry you away. Finding Shikar is only half the battle won. We still have to rescue him. You can never tell with humans. We'll wait and watch, then plan our next move.'

Down below in the hut, Chintu was upset.

'Only Rs 5000 each, Mr Pawar? That's cheating. You've sold the squirrel for Rs 5 lakhs. Surely you can give us more.'

'That's daylight robbery,' protested Arjun. 'You had promised us Rs 50,000 each.'

Mr Pawar was a short, skinny man with slitted eyes. 'Don't argue with me, boys,' he growled. 'Be happy with what you get. Five lakhs was the asking price—not what we got. People aren't dumb to pay so much for a squirrel, even if it is white-headed! The best offer we received was Rs 50,000. We've closed the deal, so that's it. Now I've paid both of you your share. Will you hand over the cage or should I take the squirrel from you forcibly?'

The cage lay on a bed to one side of the room. Chintu reluctantly crossed over to the bed and collected it.

Returning, he placed it on the table around which the men stood.

Mr Pawar and his friend Raju leaned forward, staring inside.

The cage shook as Shikar leapt, lunging at Raju's rather large nose, which was pressed against the bars. Raju, who was big and hulking, yelled and stepped back, almost falling over.

Mr Pawar grabbed the cage, lifting it. 'That's a fine specimen of a squirrel,' he said. 'Strong and healthy. Pity we are only getting Rs 50,000 for him. Come along, Raju. We have a deadline. Let's leave. We have to be back in Mumbai by evening. No deal if we don't return by then.'

'How about Rs 5000 more?' pleaded Chintu as Mr Pawar and Raju tramped out of the cottage. 'Just 5000. You can afford that. It is a fine squirrel as you said. You should pay more for him!'

Ignoring the boy, Mr Pawar walked to the van and opened the door. Shikar squeaked loudly as his cage was deposited inside. The two men settled in the vehicle and Raju cranked the engine.

There was panic in the copper pod tree.

'Kabul! We have to stop them,' cried Blackpie.

'Hold on!' squawked Snow-prise. 'Leave this to me. I can stall the humans. I've done it before. They stop in their tracks when they see me. I'll keep them occupied . . . Meanwhile, you get help, Kabul.'

With that, the paradise flycatcher swooped down. Flying boldly to the van, Snow-prise hovered in front of the windshield, in full view of the humans.

'*Oh, mere baap!*' croaked Mr Pawar. 'Look at that bird, Raju. It's beautiful! Mere baap, it's gorgeous. That's worth Rs 10,000. Switch off the engine, Raju. Switch if off, you idiot! We have nets in the car. On your feet, you lazy fellow, we *have* to catch it.'

Above, from the tree, Scarlet took to his wings. 'Come on, Bright-Jet,' he squawked. 'Snow-prise isn't the only bird who can distract humans. We can too. Let's join him!'

'That's right,' sniffed Bright-Jet. 'We are beautiful too. We'll show Snow-prise! Let's go.'

The minivets swept down from the tree and hovered beside Snow-prise.

Mr Pawar's mouth popped open, goldfish-like. 'Mere baap! This is our *matka* day, Raju. LOOK at those birds!

Ek aag jaisa, toh doosra suraj jaisa. Boys! Help us catch all three. You'll get that extra 5000 you begged for if we capture them. Come on!'

Kabul turned to her companions when the humans had leapt out of the car. 'That's great work,' she said. 'Our friends have done their job. It's up to us now. Senora, Blackpie—both of you fly to the Rose Garden. Get the human girl here. She's our best hope to rescue Shikar. Attract her attention and lead her here. I know you can do it. Make haste. Fly like falcons.'

The Rescue

Blackpie and Senora took to the skies.

Birds fly fast. There is no traffic in the skies and they cut across to their destination in a straight line. Distances that humans take forever to cover are traversed in minutes. Blackpie and Senora sped at near falcon-speed and were at the Rose Garden in little more than a minute.

Blackpie was thrilled to spot Mitalee on the lawn. There were two other humans with her—one of whom he recognized as the boy who had fired at them with his catapult. Under normal circumstances, Blackpie would have shied away, wanting nothing to do with an obvious enemy. But the circumstances were extraordinary and both Blackpie and Senora ignored the warning messages their bird-brains flashed to them. Calling loudly, they flew to Mitalee and her friends.

Alisha screamed and covered her face. Mitalee and Maitreya stared.

The birds squawked and hovered above them. Then they sped to the driveway and settled on the cycles parked there.

'Woah!' exclaimed Maitreya. 'I've never seen birds behave like that. That's so cool!'

The birds flew back to the children. Once again they fluttered before them, screeching deafeningly—louder even than babbler birds. Then they returned to the gate and the cycles.

'Cycles?' said Maitreya, scratching his head. 'Whatever do they want with our cycles?'

Mitalee said urgently, 'They are telling us something! I don't know what it is but they are trying to say something.'

The birds travelled back and forth, flying to the humans and then to the cycles.

'They . . . want us . . . to go somewhere?' said Maitreya, speaking slowly. 'Is that why they keep returning to the cycles?'

'That's it!' cried Mitalee. 'They want us to get on our cycles.' She ran forward and grabbed one. The birds immediately flew to the gate. Perching there, they stared back, calling loudly.

'We've cracked it, Mitalee!' said Maitreya. 'They want us to follow.'

'Wait for me,' she shouted. 'I'll get my bike.'

'But you're grounded,' said Alisha when Mitalee returned breathlessly with her cycle.

'Not now,' said Mitalee. 'My mother will understand. Look at the birds. Maitreya's right, they want us to follow. We have to go. Come on, let's tail them.'

The three friends mounted their bicycles. The birds flew forward and the children pedalled behind.

Back at the copper pod tree, Kabul the bulbul dropped to the roof of the van. No one was watching. Far out in the yard, the boys and the men were stalking the birds with nets in their hands. Snow-prise and the minivets had successfully diverted the humans.

The door of the van was open. Kabul hopped inside.

A joyous squeak erupted. 'KABUL!' cried Shikar.

The bulbul flew to the cage. 'Shikar! My darling squirrel! My wonderful snow-headed son! I thought I had lost you. Greatbill has been kind to me.'

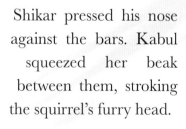

Shikar pressed his nose against the bars. Kabul squeezed her beak between them, stroking the squirrel's furry head.

'I missed you, Kabul,' whispered the squirrel, his voice breaking. 'I thought I would never ever see you again.'

'It's okay, my child,' said the bird, speaking softly. 'Kabul will never leave you. She will always be there for you. Always.'

A silence followed, deep and soulful. Time passed. The bulbul and the squirrel stood still, lost in the bliss of their reunion.

Finally, Shikar lifted his snow-white head. 'Get me out, Kabul,' he said. 'Get me out of here. I want to go back to my Rose Garden, my friends, my home.'

'You will be out soon, Shikar,' said Kabul. 'My beak cannot open your cage but help is coming. Your human friend, the girl, is on her way. I've sent Blackpie and Senora to fetch her. We will have you out soon. Don't worry. All will be fine and you will be back home.'

Although Kabul spoke confidently, Shikar sensed that all wasn't well. The bulbul's tone wasn't convincing. But the uncertainty did not dampen the squirrel's spirit. His friends were here and that was all that mattered.

'Yay!' celebrated Shikar. 'I'm finally going to be rid of this horrible cage. Blackpie won't fail us. He's a brave bird and my best friend.'

Kabul hopped to the steering wheel and peered through the windshield. Snow-prise and the minivets were flitting from tree to tree. The humans were following, moving further and further from the van. From her perch on the wheel, Kabul applauded the bravery of the birds. Speaking to Shikar, she described their successful sidetracking of the humans.

'The paradise flycatcher had warned me,' said Shikar. 'He told me not to enter the cage that terrible day, but I did not listen to him.'

'We'll talk about that later, Shikar. There's a lot you are going to hear from me. For now, I will keep you informed of what's happening outside.'

Kabul marvelled at the courage of the paradise flycatcher as she stared out across the yard. The minivets stayed high in the trees, well out of reach of the humans. But Snow-prise kept low, constantly presenting the humans a chance to snare him, keeping them interested. The bulbul watched the drama unfold.

Blackpie wished with all his little heart that the humans would move faster. It was ridiculous how slow they were! Even a cormorant with soaked wings could do better.

Senora and he squawked loudly as they flew, urging the children forward.

The three friends stayed level as they pedalled. Mitalee was the fastest. Maitreya and Alisha had to work hard to keep up with her. It was a good thing that the roads were empty. At their on-the-edge speed, they might easily have lost control dodging oncoming traffic. The yard was a considerable distance from the gardens, yet their pell-mell dash enabled them to reach it soon.

'Slow down,' cautioned Maitreya on spotting the black van. He instantly identified it as the vehicle Chintu and Arjun had been driven away in. Then he saw the boys at the far end of the yard. 'Look,' he said, pointing, 'Chintu and Arjun! They haven't seen us. Quick! Pedal to the gate. We'll hide there.'

Arriving at the gate, they dropped their cycles and crouched.

Mitalee was beside herself with excitement. 'Snowdrop is here. I *know* he's here. *Come on!* Let's go rescue him.'

Maitreya nodded. 'He should be in there. We'll sneak inside. Alisha, you wait here. Mitalee and I will check the shed out.'

'Come on!' hissed Mitalee impatiently. 'They aren't paying attention.'

Mitalee and Maitreya rose. They tiptoed through the open gate. They had barely entered the compound when a roar erupted.

'GOT HIM!' hooted Mr Pawar. 'We've got the paradise flycatcher!'

Kabul looked on in despair from the van. Snowprise's luck had run out. The net had fallen around him.

'Raju!' bawled Mr Pawar. 'Go, run to the car. Bring a cage from there. Get a large one—we want to be careful with this bird. Oh, mere baap! Oh, what a beauty he is.'

Raju turned and ran to the car. He didn't see Mitalee and Maitreya at first, but when he was halfway there, he spotted them. 'Hey!' he shouted. 'Out! Get out! This is private property.'

'Run,' said Maitreya. 'I'll tackle the man. You go and search for Snowdrop.'

'But . . .' began Mitalee. The man was big. Maitreya was no match for him.

Maitreya gave her no choice. Before she knew it, he was running towards the man. Mitalee's heart went out to Maitreya. Chintu and Arjun were coming too. It was three against one, yet Maitreya was sprinting forward undaunted.

A bird appeared as Mitalee ran. It was the bulbul. She dipped to her arm and jabbed her with her beak.

Then she flew towards the van. Mitalee had an uncanny understanding of birds. She knew instantly that the bulbul was guiding her to the vehicle. Changing direction, she raced towards it.

Maitreya could see that the man charging him was huge, the size of a bear. There was no question of engaging him in a hand-to-hand tussle. Yet, even though the man was twice his size, Maitreya believed he could tackle him. Maitreya was thin and wiry and quick on his feet. The hefty man was most certainly not. Maitreya decided upon a strategy. When the man was near, almost upon him, the boy swerved, leaping sideways. He stuck a foot out as the man lumbered past, tripping him. Raju yelped as he fell to the ground.

Meanwhile, guided by Kabul, Mitalee had reached the van. She gazed through the open door and a cry ripped from deep inside her.

'SNOWDROP!' she squealed. 'Snowdrop, my darling, beautiful Snowdrop!'

There in the cage was her most favourite creature in the whole wide world. In one swift movement, Mitalee grabbed the cage and dashed out of the van.

Out in the yard, Raju was mouthing choice curses and scrambling to his feet. Maitreya, also on the ground, was rising too. Chintu and Arjun had changed direction.

Having spied Mitalee with the cage, they were rushing towards her. Behind them, Mr Pawar had abandoned the net and the trapped bird. He was running too. The girl was stealing the squirrel! She *had* to be stopped.

Inside the cage, Shikar was squeaking with joy. Mitalee placed the cage on the ground. Kneeling, she searched for the latch.

'STOP HER!' howled Chintu.

But it was too late. Mitalee's fingers had found the latch. She flicked it back and opened the cage. Shikar leapt out of the door, his white head flashing in the sunlight.

From above, Kabul, Blackpie and Senora squawked jubilantly.

'RUN, SNOWDROP! RUN!' yelled Mitalee.

Squealing ecstatically, Shikar streaked across the yard. The birds followed, flying above him.

Mitalee ran to her cycle. Alisha lifted it, holding it for her friend.

Mr Pawar started bawling. 'Raju, catch those boys! Those *idiot* boys! The squirrel is GONE. Get my money back from them!'

Maitreya danced, waving his arms in the air, as Snowdrop raced away. Laughing, he watched as Raju grabbed Chintu and Arjun, one burly arm wrapping about each of them. He saw Mr Pawar run forward, cursing colourfully. Sweeping his gaze across the yard, Maitreya noticed that no one was paying attention to him.

When Mr Pawar had crossed him, the boy turned and sped away from the van. Running hard, he soon came to the net that trapped the paradise flycatcher. Lifting the mesh clear off the ground, he released the bird. Maitreya's mouth fell open when he saw Snow-prise take to the air. Never had he come across such a magnificent bird before. His colour was the purest white and his tail feather was long and splendid. Looking up, Maitreya saw two equally beautiful birds greet the white bird—one a dazzling shade of red and the other the colour of the sun. Together, the birds winged high, rising above the trees, and then they flew away.

Maitreya ran back to where Mitalee and Alisha were waiting. Mitalee was laughing, tears running down her face. Alisha was jumping up and down, waving her arms. He exchanged high fives and hugs with the girls.

In the yard, Mr Pawar and Raju had pinned Chintu and Arjun against the van. Raju's enormous hands were ripping Chintu's pockets off.

Chintu shouted, 'That's OUR money. How dare you take it? You gave it to us!'

'Take whatever they have,' roared Mr Pawar. 'Tear their pockets. Shred them. See that they are empty. I want every last rupee. They wasted our time and our fuel!'

Mitalee, Alisha and Maitreya shook with mirth. Chintu's cries rang in their ears as they turned their cycles.

'THIEVES . . . that's my dad's money! He gave me that 2000-rupee note!'

'Take it, Raju. That will pay for our wasted fuel.'

'GIVE IT BACK!' There was a touch of desperation in Chintu's voice. 'Dad has a terrible temper . . . Y-you d-don't know him. He'll be hopping mad! *Please*, Mr Pawar. My dad won't spare me.'

'That should serve you right,' cried Mr Pawar. 'Hope he thrashes you! You deserve it. Wasted my time. Useless boy! Now the other boy, Raju. Rip his pockets off too.'

The three friends laughed as they cycled away.

Not far ahead scampered a squirrel with a white head, joyously streaking home to his beloved Rose Garden. Above him, providing an aerial escort, flew six happy birds.

Home

'Wow!' exclaimed Maitreya, blinking. 'Am I seeing things, or what?'

The children had pedalled back to the Rose Garden. Drained by their exertions, Alisha and Maitreya were sprawled on the lawn, but Mitalee—fuelled, it seemed, by a boundless source of energy—was on her feet, dancing a jig. Maitreya was gazing at the gulmohar tree that grew behind the fountain. Since it was summer, the tree was decked with red flowers. But it wasn't the blaze of red that had prompted his utterance.

'Just look,' he continued, his eyes aglow with wonderment. 'I have never seen so many birds in my life.'

It was true. The gulmohar tree was packed with birds, so many that it seemed as though there were more birds

than flowers on the tree. And in their midst, scampering everywhere—much like an overjoyed baby—was a squirrel with a white head.

Alisha laughed. She was looking at Mitalee, who was prancing on the grass, her head turned to the gulmohar tree. Mitalee's eyes were shining and the smile on her face was as wide as Lake Neelpaani. Today the birds were not delighting Mitalee. This morning, she had eyes only for the white-headed squirrel.

Maitreya plucked a blade of grass. 'That is the most un-squirrel-like behaviour I've ever seen,' he said.

'What?' asked Alisha. 'That Snowdrop is mixing with birds?'

'Well, yes, that too. That is strange in itself—Snowdrop's friendship with birds. But what's even stranger is what he's up to. Just look at him! See how he's rubbing noses with the birds.'

'It's *beaks*, Maitreya. The birds are rubbing their beaks, and not on Snowdrop's nose. That's his forehead they are rubbing their beaks on.'

There was a lot of beak-rubbing happening. Each and every bird was stroking Snowdrop's forehead with their beak.

'That black-and-white bird,' said Maitreya, 'the one that's not leaving Snowdrop's side—that's the same bird that led us to the yard, isn't it?'

'That's right.' Alisha nodded. 'It's called a magpie-robin.'

'And that yellow bird—that's the other one, isn't it?'

'Yup. That one also led us to the yard. It's an iora. The black bird with the V-shaped tail is a drongo . . . the brown birds beside him are doves. And the green one, the one with the longish tail, is a green bee-eater!'

'What about that other one? The one I rescued. He has a really long tail. So beautiful. What's he called?'

Alisha whistled. 'Some bird, isn't he? But, um . . . I'm not sure.' She rolled on the grass, turning to Mitalee. 'What's that bird, Mitalee? That drop-dead beauty with the long tail. What's he called?'

Mitalee did not respond at first. It was only when Alisha called her name a second time and then a third that she tore her eyes away from her beloved Snowdrop.

Mitalee looked to where Alisha pointed and blinked. 'Oh my God!' she exclaimed. She hadn't been paying attention to the birds. 'The paradise flycatcher! Look! The same bird we saw in the yard.'

Alisha stared at Mitalee. 'Did you *just* notice? I mean, here's this astoundingly beautiful bird in your garden. Perched right before your eyes. He's been sitting here ever since we returned, and you didn't notice him?'

Maitreya laughed. 'Blame it on Snowdrop. Call it Snowdrop fever! Your friend's going to be weird for a while, Alisha. It's to be expected. But that gorgeous bird . . . Tell us, Mitalee. What flycatcher did you say he was?'

'Paradise,' said Mitalee. She skipped across the lawn to her friends, the Neelpaani-wide smile still plastered on her face, and squatted happily between them. 'That's a paradise flycatcher. Simply stunning. And look—there are the others. The two minivets from the yard. Right there, beside the flycatcher. See the red and yellow birds? They are minivets, scarlet minivets. The red one is the male and the yellow, the female.'

Mitalee was in high spirits. This was the happiest day of her life. But the extreme emotions of the day had taken their toll on her. Although she wanted nothing more than to skip and spin and dance the whole day, she was tired now. She sat with her friends instead, content in their company. She passed the time with them, pointing out each and every bird in the trees, identifying them particularly for Maitreya, who was keen to learn.

Above, in the gulmohar tree, Shikar was the happiest squirrel alive. He was home! Back in his beloved Rose Garden. And his friends were here. All his wonderful bird friends—and Mitalee, the human girl, too. So many beaks had been rubbed against his head that it had turned sore. Not that he cared. He was back home and that was all that mattered.

There was a great chirping and squawking and chattering from the tree. Entranced, the children sat and watched from the grass below. The sun climbed higher. The garden turned warm as the summer heat started to assert itself. It wasn't long before the birds sought shelter, seeking the more shaded sections of the garden. The children too retreated to the cooler confines of the human den. Several of the birds dispersed and the chatter amongst the branches subsided.

'Hey,' said Shikar, suddenly remembering, 'where's Mysun? I haven't seen him since I returned.'

'Amongst the flowers,' said Senora. 'Where else would he be? As if you don't know.'

'That's right,' chirped Blackpie. 'It's summertime and the flowers are blooming. Hang on, I'll find him for you.' The magpie-robin launched himself from the tree, flapping his wings.

Kabul turned to Shikar. 'No making fun of him,' warned the bulbul. 'You do know that he helped save you.'

'Yes,' twittered the iora. 'It was Mysun who told us about Snow-prise. If it weren't for him, you would still be in that horrible cage.'

There was a call from the rose bushes near the garden wall. It was Blackpie. 'He's here,' squawked the black-and-white bird.

'Be nice,' said Kabul as Shikar hopped to a branch above.

'My best behaviour,' said Shikar. 'No teasing. Promise.'

He scrambled quickly through the branches, eager to meet the sunbird.

A cheery singing greeted the squirrel as he neared the garden wall.

Summer, summer, summer,
Oh, summertime.
Ooh la la, the sun, it shines.
Summer, summer, summer,
Summertime.
Time to sing the sunbird
summer song.

Sling your beak this way, sling it
that way,
Sling it up, sling it down,
Sling it wherever you want.
All you see is flowers,
Flowers everywhere.
Hollyhocks, pansies, petunias,
Zinnias, roses, hibiscus.
The sky, the sun, the flowers, all in
bloom.
Oh, yeah, it's the sunbird season,
It's summertime.

Summer, summer, summer,
Summertime, flower-time.
Summer, summer, summer,
Time to sing the sunbird summer song.

Gulmohar, silk and forest flame,
Fire in the trees—

'HEY, MYSUN!' Shikar chattered loudly.

Mysun's song ended abruptly. The sunbird backed away from the red rose he had been caressing with his beak. His feathers sparkled as he hovered angrily.

'Shikar!' he screeched, spying the squirrel. 'That was rude. Don't squirrels have any manners? You interrupted my song—and my feeding too.'

'Mysun! Mysun—my dear friend. I'm back. I'm here. I'm home!'

'I've got eyes, you know. I can see you're here.' Mysun glowered at Shikar. 'It's *you* who doesn't have eyes. Can't you see I'm feeding? Now, will you let me be?'

With that, the sunbird turned away and sank his beak in another rose.

Blackpie swept forward. 'Mysun, Shikar is back! You saved him.'

'Eh?' The sunbird turned to Blackpie. 'Me? *I* saved somebody? Did I?'

Blackpie stared at Mysun. Then an idea struck him. Turning, he squawked loudly, 'Snow-prise! Snow-prise, come here, please.'

'Sure,' twittered a bird from the gulmohar tree. 'Coming.'

Blackpie dropped to the garden wall. Shikar leapt on to it too. Snow-prise joined them, touching down between the squirrel and the robin.

Mysun gazed at Snow-prise. His long, curved beak opened and clicked shut several times. Paradise flycatchers are handsome birds. Other birds often stop and admire them. But it wasn't Snow-prise's looks that were drawing Mysun's attention.

'The flycatcher!' squawked the sunbird, his berry-sized brain working furiously. 'I remember you. The hibiscus! You were here when the hibiscus bush was blooming. And Shikar, you were with—' Mysun halted midsentence. He gazed at Shikar, his eyes expanding till they were the size of chikoo seeds. 'SHIKAR!' screeched the sunbird. 'Oh, Greatbill be thanked. Shikar is back. My dear squirrel friend is back!'

Mysun shot forward to where the squirrel sat and, hovering beside him, rubbed his beak on Shikar's aching head.

'Oh!' crooned Snow-prise. 'Another sweet reunion. This garden is something else. Where does all this love here spring from?'

Kabul, Senora and the minivets winged over too, adding to the happy collection of creatures on the wall.

Shikar and Mysun huddled close. The squirrel stroked the sunbird's feathered cheek with his nose. 'Thanks, Mysun. Kabul told me the whole story. If it weren't for you, I wouldn't be back here. You saved me. I won't ever forget it.'

The sunbird's chest swelled with pride. 'I'm intelligent,' he said. 'I always knew I was.'

Kabul nodded. 'You *are* intelligent, Mysun. You are brave too.'

Mysun's chest expanded even more, till it looked like it might burst. But as he opened his beak to speak, there was a loud squeak from a tree in the Leaf Garden.

Shikar reacted instantly. He leapt from the wall into the Leaf Garden. Speeding across the grass, he dashed up the trunk of a jamun tree. There were two squirrels high up on a branch. Shikar scampered to where they waited and flung himself in their midst.

'Aw,' said Senora.

'His squirrel friends, Supari and Paan,' said Kabul.

'Isn't he happy to be back with them?'

The three squirrels were clinging to one another tightly, like a ball. A loud, happy chattering rang from them.

'Another reunion,' sighed Snow-prise.

'See, I told you, Shikar is sweet on Supari,' said Blackpie.

'Now, now,' said Kabul, 'let's not start—'

But the bulbul did not complete her sentence. She had noticed movement near the human den of the Leaf Garden. Chintu, the horrible boy, had entered the gate.

'Blackpie,' hissed the bulbul. 'Look!'

The magpie-robin turned.

The birds saw Chintu step on to the grassy lawn and halt. He had heard the chattering, because his head was turned and he was looking up.

Chintu was in a dishevelled state. His shirt was crumpled and streaked with mud, and the pockets of his pants seemed to have come loose. They were dangling, like tufts of soiled grass, on his hips.

High up in the jamun tree, Shikar's white head was clearly visible. Kabul saw Chintu stiffen. The boy stared for a long time before lowering his eyes. His gaze then swept over the Leaf Garden, before coming to rest on a wooden table at its centre.

Chintu seemed to flinch as he looked at the table. Its surface was covered with small wine glasses, placed out in the sun to dry. Chintu swallowed, knowing he was in trouble. It had been his job to wash the glasses. His mother had instructed him to do so. But he had postponed the chore, planning to do it after his meeting with Mr Pawar. What Chintu hadn't counted on was being made to trek back from the yard, as Mr Pawar had forced him to do. After a long, exhausting walk, he had finally returned. But it was too late. The glasses were already washed. He was in trouble.

The squirrel chatter from the tree attracted his attention again. This time when he spied Shikar's white head, his heart beat faster. That awful squirrel! The creature behind all his troubles! Chintu's spiteful mind conjured an image of his catapult. Yes . . . the catapult!

It was in his room. It would enable him to get even with that horrible animal. Chintu strode inside.

Kabul sensed trouble.

But it was Blackpie who spoke first. 'I have an idea,' he squawked. 'Follow me.'

The magpie-robin winged to the table. Dropping low, he grabbed one of the tiny glasses in his beak and then rose into the air. Kabul instantly understood the robin's plan.

'Come,' she called to the other birds. 'Do as Blackpie has done. All of you. Collect those hunkins* and fly high.'

Winging to the table, the birds each collected a glass and flapped skyward. It wasn't easy. The glasses were heavy, particularly for a small bird like Senora. But she flapped hard and rose alongside her companions.

By the time Chintu returned, catapult in hand, the birds were fluttering high above the table.

Up in the sky, Blackpie looked around him. The minivets, Snow-prise, Kabul and Senora hovered beside him, a glass held fast in each of their beaks. On the ground below, Chintu was loading his catapult, his eyes fixed on the jamun tree.

---

* Objects belonging to humans.

'Now!' hissed Blackpie, letting go of his glass. The other birds released theirs too. It took just a couple of seconds, no more. There was an ear-splitting crash as the glasses fell to the table. They shattered instantly, smashing the others on the tabletop too.

Chintu jumped on hearing the sound. Loud shouts came from inside his home.

'What's that?' It was Chintu's father.

'My glasses!' gasped his mother. 'My beautiful glasses. Oh no!'

Chintu's mother came rushing out. Her eyes shrank with horror when she saw the table. Her precious glasses were smashed—all of them—their fragments catching the sunlight on the lawn. Lifting her gaze, she saw Chintu standing beside the table, catapult in hand.

'YOU!' screeched his mother. 'You *terrible* boy. You did this!'

'*Me?* No, I didn't, Mother!'

'Yes, you did! With that horrible catapult of yours. Give that to me. Give it to me now!'

'No-no! Mom, it wasn't me. Promise.'

'They just exploded on their own, did they?' barked Chintu's father, who had stepped out too.

'I-I-I . . . Mom, Dad, it wasn't me!'

'You rascal,' ranted his mother. 'First you disobey me—you don't wash the glasses when you were instructed to. Then you smash them. And look at you! What have you done to your pockets?'

Chintu dropped his catapult. His hands fell to the ripped pockets that dangled at his hips, trying desperately to cover them.

'My money!' roared his dad. 'Two thousand rupees that I gave you to buy the lights. Has my money gone with your pockets? WHERE'S THE MONEY?'

Anger blazed in the man's eyes. Unable to hold his father's gaze, Chintu looked away. He turned to the Rose Garden wall and blinked. Mitalee, Alisha and Maitreya were standing there. They were staring and laughing at him. Wow-Wow was there too, his tongue hanging to one side.

'You there,' hollered Chintu's father, pointing at Maitreya. 'You're his friend, aren't you? Do you know what he did with my money?'

'Friend, huh?' whispered Mitalee.

Maitreya winked at her. 'I'm on this side of the fence today, aren't I?' Then he looked at Chintu's dad. 'Yes, I do know what Chintu did with the money, Uncle. He gave it all to a man this morning. I saw him.'

Chintu's dad had turned red. Froth was collecting at his mouth. His lips were twitching. The words were coming out, but they were strained and low.

'You . . . you gave away my money . . .?'

Chintu's mother turned away from her broken crockery. She looked at the children, a grim expression on her face. 'Did you see him break the glasses?' she asked.

'No, Auntie,' replied Mitalee. 'We heard them breaking. It made such an awful noise, so we came running. But Chintu keeps using that catapult of his. I've seen him hurt birds and animals.'

The garden turned silent. It was an ominous silence. Chintu's parents glared at their son. The expression on their faces wasn't of the loving variety. Far from it. Suddenly a whimper filled the garden, echoing everywhere. It was a pathetic grovelling whine, the kind Wow-Wow often made. Mitalee looked at the dog. But the sound wasn't coming from him.

It was Chintu.

His father was pointing at the house. Chintu walked, his moaning turning steadily louder, swelling to a wail by the time he entered. His parents followed, slamming the door shut behind them.

The three friends burst into laughter. Wow-Wow barked. Six birds flew low—in formation, like fighter jets—and swept above the children's heads. In the jamun tree, three squirrels gazed happily at one another. And in the rose bushes, a bird sang in a bright, sunny voice.

Summer, summer, summer,
Oh, summertime.
Ooh la la, the sun, it shines.
  Summer, summer, summer,
  Summertime.
    Time to sing the sunbird summer
    song.